Sherbet

Volume One

Writer/Co-Creator: Michael Vincent Bramley   Artist/Co-Creator: Joshua Mathus

Colours: Rosemary Cheetham   Cover Artist: Alice Meichi Li

Variant Cover Artist: Hyeondo Park

Logo Design: Jared Fletcher

Cpoy Eidtor: Ken Ip

SHERBET VOLUME 1. First Printing September 2015, ISBN: 978-0-692-52379-7. Stories from this book have been previously published online for hadroncolliderscope.com (2009/2010), in magazine form as Sherbet: 2011 Halloween Special, Sherbet: 2012 Summer Special and ebook form as Sherbet: 2014 Digital Special. Copyright © Michael Vincent Bramley and Joshua Mathus 2009, 2010, 2011, 2012, 2014, 2015. Sherbet Lock and all supporting characters are trademarks of Michael Vincent Bramley and Joshua Mathus. All characters are fictitious and any resemblance to persons alive or dead is purely coincidental (except for in instances of satire, or where fictionalized versions of Kickstarter backers have been featured as rewards for pledges).

LONDON ST. BAKER CITY

Spending several hours a day beneath an underwear model SOUNDED like my idea of a good time, but baby; you gotta read that fine print.

(That was a joke.)

I'll say this about living in London St., you never know who's going to come knocking on your door.

ENTER.

FANTASTIC. There are few things sexier than a desperate lady in a wide-rimmed hat.

Detective Lock, I tried emailing you, but when I didn't get a response...

Well, it is just of the *utmost* imperative that we speak; my darling husband has been *KIDNAPPED.*

KIDNAPPED? Oh *my, my... please* elaborate.

Please, don't act like you're enjoying this. My beloved Desmynd is missing and these... *BEASTS mutilated* him.

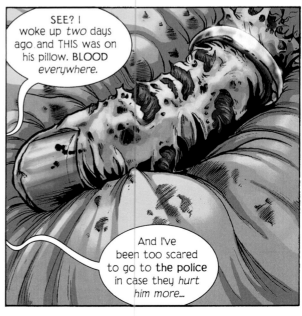

SEE? I woke up *two* days ago and THIS was on his pillow. BLOOD *everywhere.*

And I've been too scared to go to the police in case they *hurt him more...*

"Don't remember it?"

"No doubt. Lycanthropes *rarely* remember anything of their other lives once they've reverted to *human form.*"

"I'm sure your husband *tried* to find you in those animal eyes, but you were just a *wolf,* tearing him *to pieces.*"

"I doubt you had to leave the room. You just ate until you were full and then *passed out* satisfied..."

"You didn't even stop until you tasted silver and promptly *spat out* that finger."

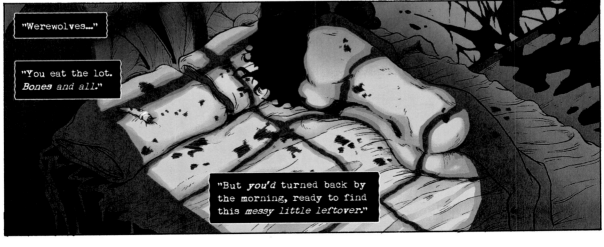

"Werewolves..."

"You eat the lot. *Bones* and all."

"But *you'd* turned back by the morning, ready to find this *messy little leftover.*"

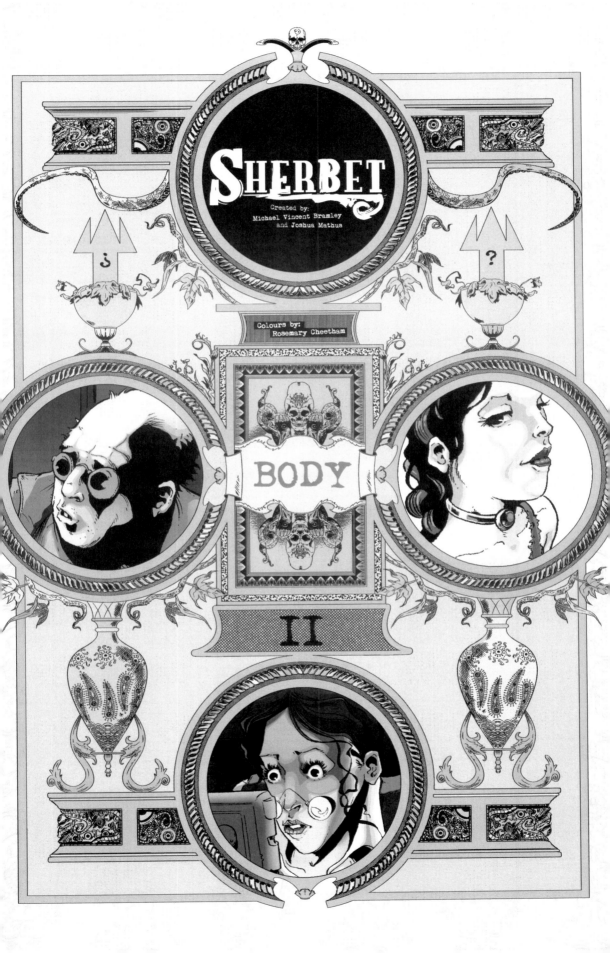

LONDON ST. BAKER CITY

My client, Iain Dobbs, smells awful and has the air of a Subway flasher about him.

My sexy, young girlfriend is missing and *no one else remembers her!*

He might also be a pathological liar.

"No, really, Agatha lived in the flat next door to me, we'd meet on our way back from work."

"One thing led to another... and... well, you know..."

WHOOREZ!!

SPIRITS! LEAVE THIS PLACE!

"It was going great until a *kid* from the downstairs flat got *possessed* and they called in *a priest."*

"The exorcism *was* successful, but when I got home that day, Agatha's door was *gone."*

"SHE was gone."

"Now *no one* even remembers her, not even the landlords."

"I think that whatever possessed that boy kidnapped my Agatha and *dragged her to hell,* but no one will even listen to me."

They all say I'm crazy!

Now *all I have left* is this photo she gave me...

Your story has touched me deeply, *Mr. Dobbs*. I'll do what I can.

I thought Iain was as *delusional* as he was *off-putting*, but telling him that would only prolong his stay, so I *tried* to placate him.

BUT, if true... this could be my own '*Phantom Room*' case. My mind was giddy with thoughts of witches and false dimensions.

Agatha's flat WAS in the building plans. It *HAD* existed. Something had eaten it up, or concealed it somehow.

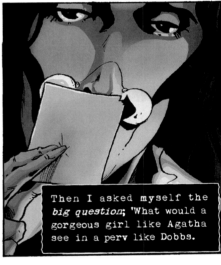

Then I asked myself the *big question*; 'What would a gorgeous girl like Agatha see in a perv like Dobbs.

Venturing into the city newspaper archives yielded no worthwhile results, until I thought to broaden the *search parameters*.

JESUS CHRIST ON A FUCKING BOUNCY CASTLE!

Suddenly, *it all started to make sense.*

Think of her as a *REALLY old* cougar if that makes you *feel* any better?

HurRGKGK!

Agatha vanished *over 70 years ago.* She'd been seeing Flint Gurney, former owner of this building.

Years later *Shoggoth Yard* found *another* of Flint's girlfriends walled up in another flat he owned, just like this one.

He was *shanked* to death in prison.

Strangely no one went looking for Agatha.

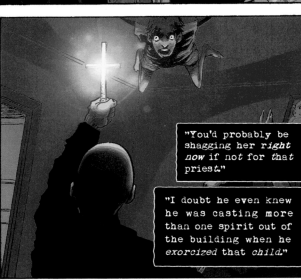

"You'd probably be shagging her *right now* if *not* for *that* priest."

"I doubt he even knew he was casting more than one spirit out of the building when he *exorcized* that *child.*"

If you ever DID care about the poor girl; take solace in the fact that *this is good for her.*

Oh... God... it's so disgusting... God...

Ah yes. I expected you'd *feel* that way.

Christ Iain. It's all about *YOU* isn't it.

I hate being anyone's performing monkey, but sometimes it is *unavoidable*.

For instance, when *Shoggoth's* *'Finest'* crash into your office and catch you *RED HANDED*.

MISSING

Or *WHITE NOSED*.

In these cases, it's wise to put on your *best monkey dance* until it all blows over.

LAMB'S HEAD ROW. BAKER CITY

Tch... what a shithole.

KUNT

Tristan and Josie Darwin, I am *D.I Lestrade*, this is *D. I. Gregson* and I'd also like to introduce you to *Sherbet*.

Don't let the stripper's name fool you, she's an outside consultant and she's *very good*.

PLEASE! YOU *HAVE* TO HELP US FIND MY LITTLE GIRL, SHE *NEVER DID NUFFIN'* WRONG!

Hang on... your son has nightmares about a *scary stranger* in his room and you ignore him. *OK.*

But your little princess vanishes and you don't think to reassess his claims?

Oh yeah, *'DARWIN'*, that name isn't ironic at all, is it?

Get them out of here, boys. Leave the kid.

Right-o then Andy... Why not tell me what *you* saw?

FUK

It sounded so silly...

A *BOGEYMAN* keeps coming in... he scratches at the window when Belinda is asleep. Then the room goes all *green* and *foggy...*

It stinks like CHEESE, or *summink.*

"When the fog goes, he's sittin' on her, telling her to do *bad things.*"

"She used to be nice to me, but since he started coming she's been so mean."

A bogeyman. No documented cases in *CENTURIES...*

THE OLD BOWERY, BAKER CITY

I think of it as *assisted suicide.*

There have been no recorded sightings of bogeymen in centuries. They were long thought extinct.

Must be *lonely.*

'STRANGERSON DAIRY BOTTLING' was the largest source of milk and *dairy products* in a city of 20 million.

Where are the workers?

WHERE THE HELL IS THIS **MILK** EVEN FROM?

The milk all came from the same terrible place.

I'll warn you here, some doors are best left closed. *Sometimes* you don't want to know what's behind them.

I'll let you decide for yourself.

PRIVATE

Go ahead. Open it. If you NEED to know.

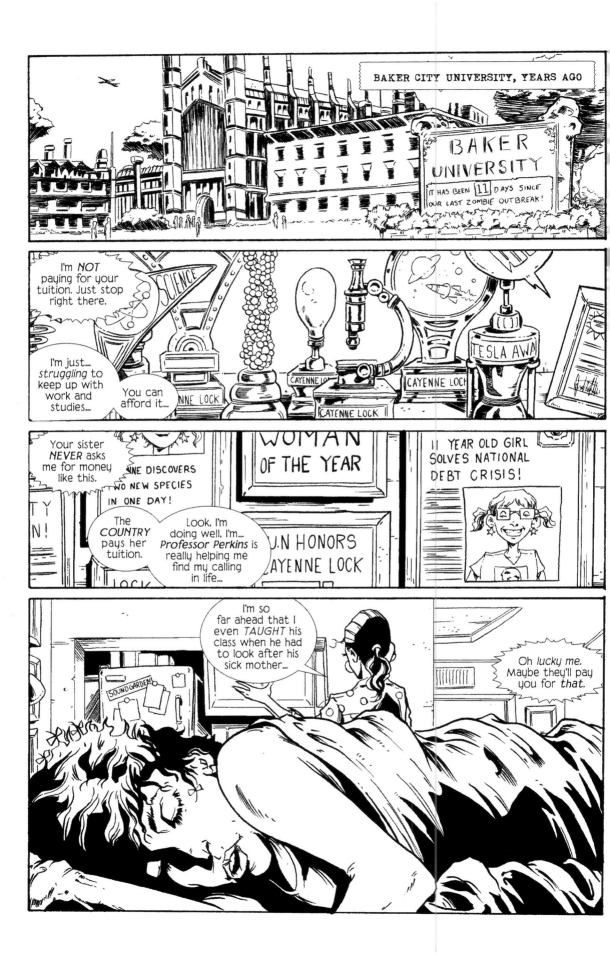

CAYENNE!

Whassat?

WHY IS THERE A *MONKEY* IN THE FRIDGE?

Oh him... *Georgey* is cooling off.

His mood helmet overheated and got stuck on *'Rage'*.

Don't worry about it.

Hey! Let's go get breakfast.

Seriously? It's *7PM*, Cayenne!

"Ooh... Okie-doke! How about **DINNER** then?"

THE BURNT CRUMPE

THIS BUILDING IS NOT ZOMBIE PROOF!

They're keeping to one side right now, so if we run we can make it.

Just try to keep up with me, OK?

Okie doke... lead the way!

Pant...

Pant...

HEY!

What is he looking f-

OH *OF COURSE!*

You're coming with me!

'WHY IS THERE A MONKEY
IN THE FRIDGE?'

NAG'S TAIL HILLS, OUTER-BAKER

Are you Sherbet? The d-d-detective?

Why yes, *d-d-Dr.* Foster.

DR MALCOLM FOSTER

What *exactly* is so important that *I* had to come to see *you?*

This place is badly h-haunted, but I *c-c-c-can't* l-l-leave. *M-my* research is *too* important.

What makes you think you have a *ghost* here?

M-M-MALCOLM YOU FRAUD!

Aha! Very astute.

It *KILLS* you, Malcolm.

"An exact copy comes waltzing out of 'BOOTH B', a copy of the body *AND* of the soul."

"The ORIGINAL soul of the dead you remains in *the first booth.*"

"And the jealous fucker thinks you stole its life, because *YOU DID!*"

"And... shit, if the exorcist took care of *ONE* ghost already, then it means you used the booths *AGAIN!*"

GOOD GOD, *HOW MANY TIMES,* MALCOLM?!

'Like... I know about goblins, ghosts and all that, but... aliens? Bullshit, right?'

NIBELUNG GLOBAL BANK
BAKER CITY

Operator? Karen Hsieh in Baker City please.

Karen? I'm going to be really late home. There's too much fog.

I just know I won't be able to land until it clears.

Uhuh. I'll be fine... *you too...*

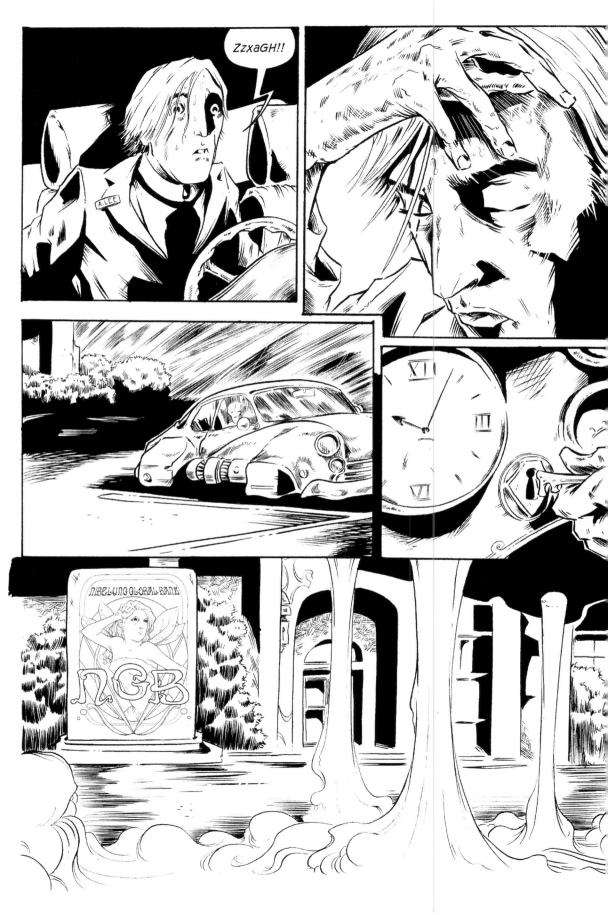

I don't follow.

I bought him this shirt... or *one* of these. He only had one. Now he has *two*. And *look*...

He *tore* that sleeve the first time he wore it and I sewed it up that night.

Uncanny.

It's the same mend down to the *stitching*. It's the same shirt.

There's the same loose thread, *same* chip on the second to last button... identical *except*...

Would you look at *that*?

SHOGGOTH YARD
BAKER CITY

ALIENS!

ALIENS ABDUCTED ME! YOU **HAVE** TO BELIEVE ME!

BEDLAM

You have to believe me! My name is *Brandon Montclare*! I need to get home to my wife!

SHADDAP! We called the number, *nutcase*! The REAL **Brandon Montclare** picked up his phone!

That *name*...

That's not me! It must be an imposter! An *alien plant!*

Listen **Bird-Bloke**, if some *Duke* needs a new *vital organ*, that's serious business, but we haven't had any deaths lately. Although **'Batshit Brandon'** in there is technically a *John Doe*. He's doing my head in with all this 'alien' shite. Hows about I just *turn my back* for five minutes?

You want a coffee? Cigarette? Some *blow*?

I'm good... *thanks*?

In your own words, why don't you tell me what happened?

At first I thought it was a nightmare, but I think I actually was *abducted* by *aliens*.

They took me to their ship and pulled me apart and when I woke up... when I got back things had changed here.

Karen had changed.

I think she's under *their* control.

Why do... why do you need me in here? *Am I under arrest*?

No, no. I just need to ask you some questions about *your relationship*.

OK... I *suppose*.

How did you meet?

I was part of the *Asia Pacific Affairs Council* at *Hyde University*... He turned up for the welcome event... I looked him up online later.

We met at the welcome event for the Asia Pacific Affairs Council at *Hyde*, of which she was chair. She found me online months later.

First Kiss?

I was staying at his flat for the first time, it just happened naturally.

We first kissed when she stayed at my flat for the first time.

Why did you move here last year?

I moved here for *work* and Alex followed me so we could be together.

We moved in to stay together after I finished my *grad program*, while she was already working here.

What was the last big family event you *both* attended?

Well, it'd be his dad's birthday. We went to *Big Moose Lake* last October to celebrate with his family.

I'm not sure off hand. We were meant to go to *Big Moose Lake* last October for dad's birthday, but Karen and I got *food poisoning*...

"It is now MY theory that 'timeslip' has less to do with time travel and more to do with traveling laterally to parallel realities where time is a little ahead or behind."

"This time the differences between realities were bigger and didn't go unnoticed."

"Alex remembers them experimenting on him. Who knows how long for? Then they either dumped him here thinking no one would notice, or..."

"Well, it's not a comfortable thought, but maybe THIS is the real experiment."

"How would we KNOW?"

"That said, I don't know what kind of aliens we're dealing with. I'm predominantly basing my assumptions on one book I've read detailing medieval encounters with the 'Little Green Men'."

Therefore, I don't have much data on them that would explain their motivations.

I don't think we'll *ever* know for sure.

"It's patchy at best. These kinds of alien tactics make the **victim** seem insane. Unreliable."

Kriztille? Get me the Commander would you?

'Ello M'am. You said to call if I had updates on the loon we threw in *Bedlam* this morning.

Turns out he was abducted, according to *Lock*, so we turfed him out.

Thank you Gregory, that will be all. "*We are the Shoggoth. Where are our eyes?*"

"*Everywhere.*"

Oh, I also found my missing I.D, it was in my pocket all al- ⟩CLICK⟨

You heard the fool, ladies and gentleman.

I'm opening the floor to *thoughts and suggestions.*

'I'm starting to sense a pattern here.'

'Luckily cocaine is a
natural anaesthetic.'

LONDON STREET

Where's *Tweedle-dee*?

Are you hurt, Sherbet?

Concerned about me, are you? I'm *touched*.

Luckily cocaine is a natural anaesthetic.

What do you want, Gregson?

I want to know what you've gotten yourself into this time.

Walk with me, I'll tell you what I know.

Your little *Shoglets* here tell me that it was an accident. The steering locked up.

But I SAW the cab swoop around that Church like there was some force repelling it.

"It's as though the poor bastard driving was trying to pull up, but the cab was magnetically DRAWN to Eugene..."

...moments after I mockingly convinced him that this exact thing wouldn't happen...

So what now? We go find this psychic woman?

No, not yet.

I want to know what we're dealing with.

Whuah?

Why are we in muh bar?

We know about the Demon you smuggled into the city, Seamus.

The nasty in that Fairlop Urn,,,

SATURDAY IS DEMON NIGHT! SUCCUBI DRINK **FREE!**

DEMON? Are you insinuatin' that *Aul' Seamus* would cavort with *FALLEN ANGELS*? The VERY IDEA!

Why... I've never even *MET* a demon!

C'mon, that's just embarrassing, Seamus.

Did you KNOW what was in that Urn you sold? A *Wahnsin-nteuffel*. You know what they are capable of?

Fffeck.

Feckin' fine then.

But *Fairlop Oak* is *extinct* in *this* dimension and we *lesser fae* ain't exactly welcomed back to *Faerie* wi' open arms.

A *Cadmus* Fixing Curse on a normal bottle traps *most* demons...

'You really need to forget about those carrot sticks...'

This city *especially*.

Just last week I saw a *comatose woman* with a *hole in her gut* where her... well *her baby*... I guess it *ate* its way out.

The doctors had no idea how or WHY she was *still alive*.

We read about all this madness and it's tempting to believe when a loved one passes that some *larger force* is at play.

Trust me, though; the simplest answers still tend to be the right ones. Even in *this* climate.

If you'd just — *just* do an autopsy, you'll see; he didn't drink.

Oh I'm very sorry, but by now *the Birdmen* have been at him.

I TRULY am very sorry for your loss.

BAKER CITY UNIVERSITY, HOME OF THE LOCK TWINS

It's SUPER useful!

OK, first of all, *no it isn't*, and secondly... no... *actually...*

I'm still hung up on that first point. What is useful about a weapon that gives people *amnesia*?

It's not a weapon, silly. *I told you already,* People say ignorance is bliss, so I'm making the world a better place!

One bullet at a-

I don't remember you telling me that. *Why don't I remember you telling me that*?!

It works! *YAY!*

I wouldn't complain if I were you, *darling*, it seems like you need ME to do YOUR dark things for you.

You two are into some *dark* things, aren't you.

I've seen all I need to see here.

Let's get out of here before some other forgetful sod wanders in.

Already? What did you find?

The damage here isn't at all conducive with landing from a fall, he was *crushed* by something big.

First thing tomorrow, we let the Chancellor of the BCU know that there's a GIANT *killing* students in the Staggered Wood.

We might not have more time. This thing is alive and it's killing people.

Miyoko and I are going to go out later to find something we can show the Chancel-

GREAZsh!

Are you coming to the woods with us or not?

We're looking for a trail... broken trees, anything blue and paint-like, or failing that anything *humongous and deadly.*

I wanted you to know, I really appreciate all of this...

Cayenne, I know you don't know me too well and I didn't even know you had a twin sister until yesterday...

Aww, don't mention it!

And Sharbs pretends to be prickly, but she *loves* helping really. She's been so bored since her course got *cancelled*...

Because of the *Perkins* thing? I did hear about it.

She's right, I'm here because I'm bored. I'm still wondering why YOU'RE here though.

NO!

GEOORRRGE!

He's *DEAD*, Cayenne! Let it GO!

Chancellor
Deborah Lansley

GIANT OF BCU

BCU Closed Down After Student Deat Cover Up

Chancellor Implicated i Doll-Based Ecstasy Smuggling Ring!

Three Days Later

"When police tried to interview Lansley about the giant, she tried to make her escape *via the window*."

"They found $200k and 14 kilos of ecstasy hidden in her office crawlspace linking her to an unrelated *drug-trafficking ring*."

Oh... hi.

Hello Miyoko. Looks like we destroyed the school.

Want to sit with me for a bit?

Um... I think that depends. I've got some questions I wanted to ask you.

Oh. THIS. Yes, the rumours are true, I *AM* a lesbian.

No, not tha- *wait really*? No. Never mind, I had more important questions.

Like...?

The *paramedics* are on the way.

Paramedics? You mean *vultures*.

What on earth they expect to harvest from *this freak*, I have no idea.

Hey... Why would *Andres Aguirre* be travelling with *the Birdmen*?

Mayor.

Detective. Have your men clear out. We'll take it from here.

COVERS

PIN-UPS

& SKETCHES

ALICE MEICHI LI

ALICE MEICHI LI

HYEONDO P

KATELAN FOISY

JASON LOO

SHAKY KANE

MARCUS MULLER

ALAN RYAN

ZAWADI NOEL

GLENN FABRY 2015

GLENN FABRY

JOSH MATHUS

SIMON FRAS

ROB MORAN

PAUL HANLEY

YAO XIAO

LEILA DEL DUCA

JOSH MATHUS

LISANDRO DI PASQUALE

DIPASQUALE

JOSH MATHUS

ALLY CAT

PAIGE! 2013

PAIGE PUMPHREY

DELIA GABLE

KRIZTILLE JUNIO

D. YEE

NATASHA SANDERS

STEVIE WILSON

N. STEVEN HARRIS

KRISTEN TERRANA-HOLLIS

JOSH MATHUS